MY LITTLE PONY

Friendship is Magic

VOL. 2

WRITTEN BY **Katie Cook**

ART BY **Andy Price**

COLORS BY **Heather Breckel**

LETTERS BY **Robbie Robbins** and **Neil Uyetake**

EDITED BY **Bobby Curnow**

 Spotlight

 IDW

ABDOPUBLISHING.COM

Reinforced library bound edition published in 2016 by Spotlight,
a division of ABDO, PO Box 398166, Minneapolis, Minnesota 55439.
Spotlight produces high-quality reinforced library bound editions for
schools and libraries. Published by agreement with IDW.

Printed in the United States of America, North Mankato, Minnesota.
042015
092015

 THIS BOOK CONTAINS
RECYCLED MATERIALS

Licensed By:

LIBRARY OF CONGRESS CATALOGING-IN-PUBLICATION DATA

Cook, Katie, 1981-
  My little pony : friendship is magic / writer, Katie Cook ; artist, Andy Price ;
colors, Heather Breckel ; letters, Robbie Robbins and Neil Uyetake. --
Reinforced library bound edition.
    8 volumes ; cm
  Volumes 1-4 written by Katie Cook, illustrated by Andy Price -- Volumes 5-8
written by Heather Nuhfer, illustrated by Amy Mebberson.
  ISBN 978-1-61479-376-2 (v. 1) -- ISBN 978-1-61479-377-9 (v. 2) --
ISBN 978-1-61479-378-6 (v. 3) -- ISBN 978-1-61479-379-3 (v. 4) --
ISBN 978-1-61479-380-9 (v. 5) -- ISBN 978-1-61479-381-6 (v. 6) --
ISBN 978-1-61479-382-3 (v. 7) -- ISBN 978-1-61479-383-0 (v. 8)
  1. Graphic novels. I. Price, Andy, illustrator. II. Nuhfer, Heather, author. III.
Mebberson, Amy ; illustrator. IV. My little pony, friendship is magic (Television
program) V. Title. VI. Title: Friendship is magic.
  PZ7.7.C666My 2016
  741.5'973--dc23
                    2015001976

Spotlight

A Division of ABDO
abdopublishing.com

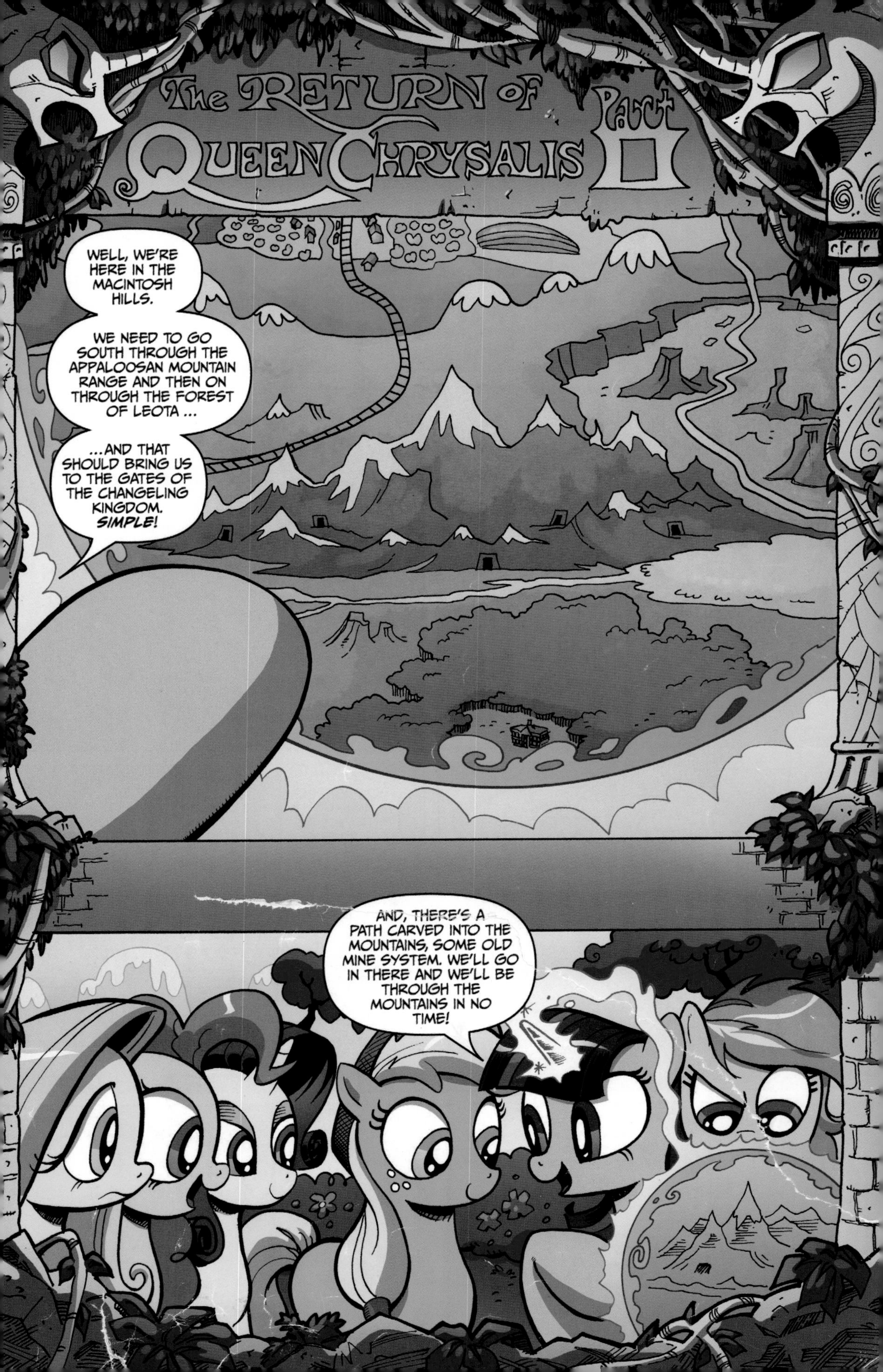
The Return of Queen Chrysalis
Part II
WELL, WE'RE HERE IN THE MACINTOSH HILLS.
WE NEED TO GO SOUTH THROUGH THE APPALOOSAN MOUNTAIN RANGE AND THEN ON THROUGH THE FOREST OF LEOTA ...
...AND THAT SHOULD BRING US TO THE GATES OF THE CHANGELING KINGDOM. SIMPLE!
AND, THERE'S A PATH CARVED INTO THE MOUNTAINS, SOME OLD MINE SYSTEM. WE'LL GO IN THERE AND WE'LL BE THROUGH THE MOUNTAINS IN NO TIME!

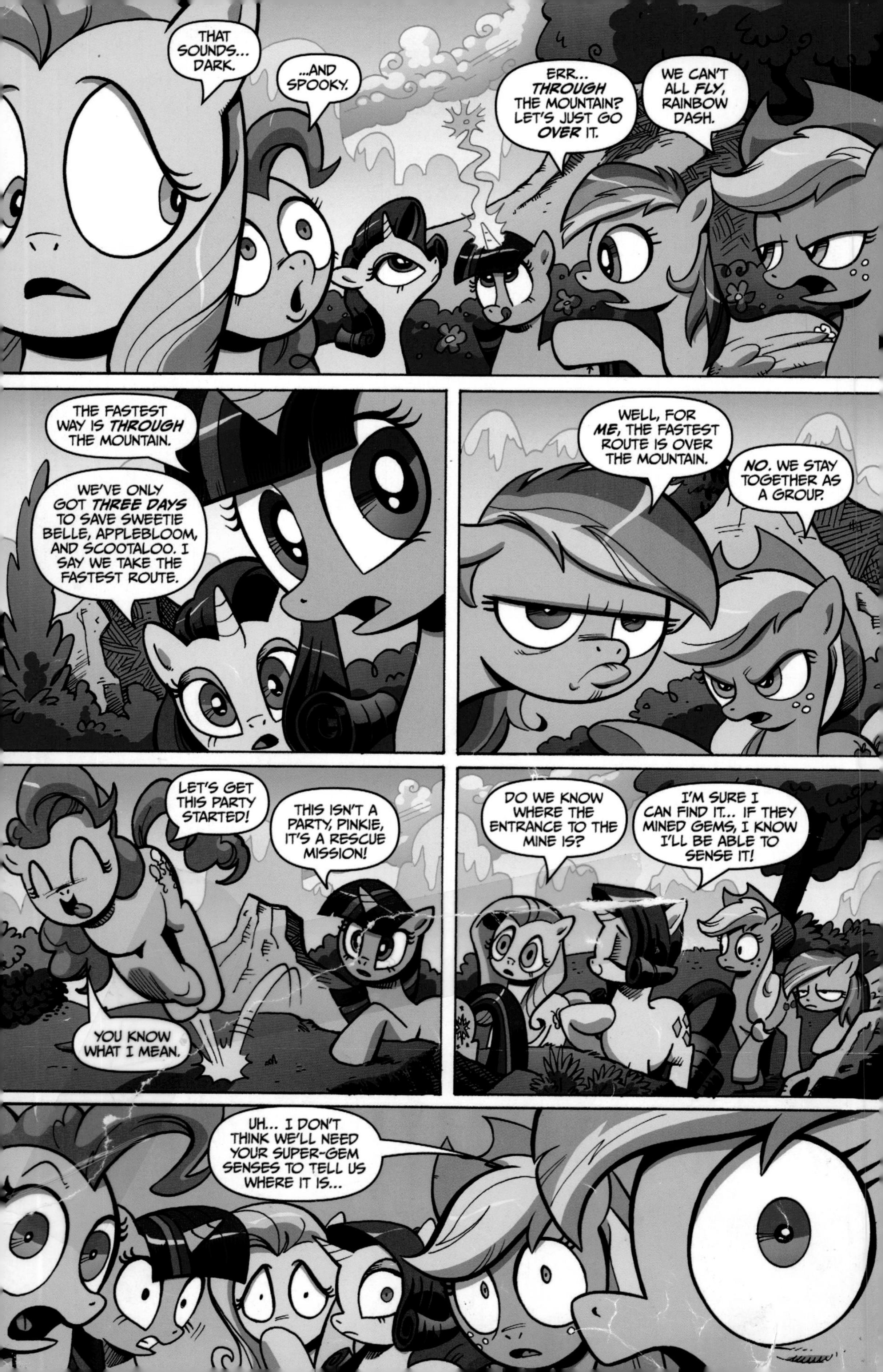
THAT SOUNDS... DARK.
...AND SPOOKY.
ERR... THROUGH THE MOUNTAIN? LET'S JUST GO OVER IT.
WE CAN'T ALL FLY, RAINBOW DASH.
THE FASTEST WAY IS THROUGH THE MOUNTAIN.
WE'VE ONLY GOT THREE DAYS TO SAVE SWEETIE BELLE, APPLEBLOOM, AND SCOOTALOO. I SAY WE TAKE THE FASTEST ROUTE.
WELL, FOR ME, THE FASTEST ROUTE IS OVER THE MOUNTAIN.
NO. WE STAY TOGETHER AS A GROUP.
LET'S GET THIS PARTY STARTED!
THIS ISN'T A PARTY, PINKIE, IT'S A RESCUE MISSION!
YOU KNOW WHAT I MEAN.
DO WE KNOW WHERE THE ENTRANCE TO THE MINE IS?
I'M SURE I CAN FIND IT... IF THEY MINED GEMS, I KNOW I'LL BE ABLE TO SENSE IT!
UH... I DON'T THINK WE'LL NEED YOUR SUPER-GEM SENSES TO TELL US WHERE IT IS...

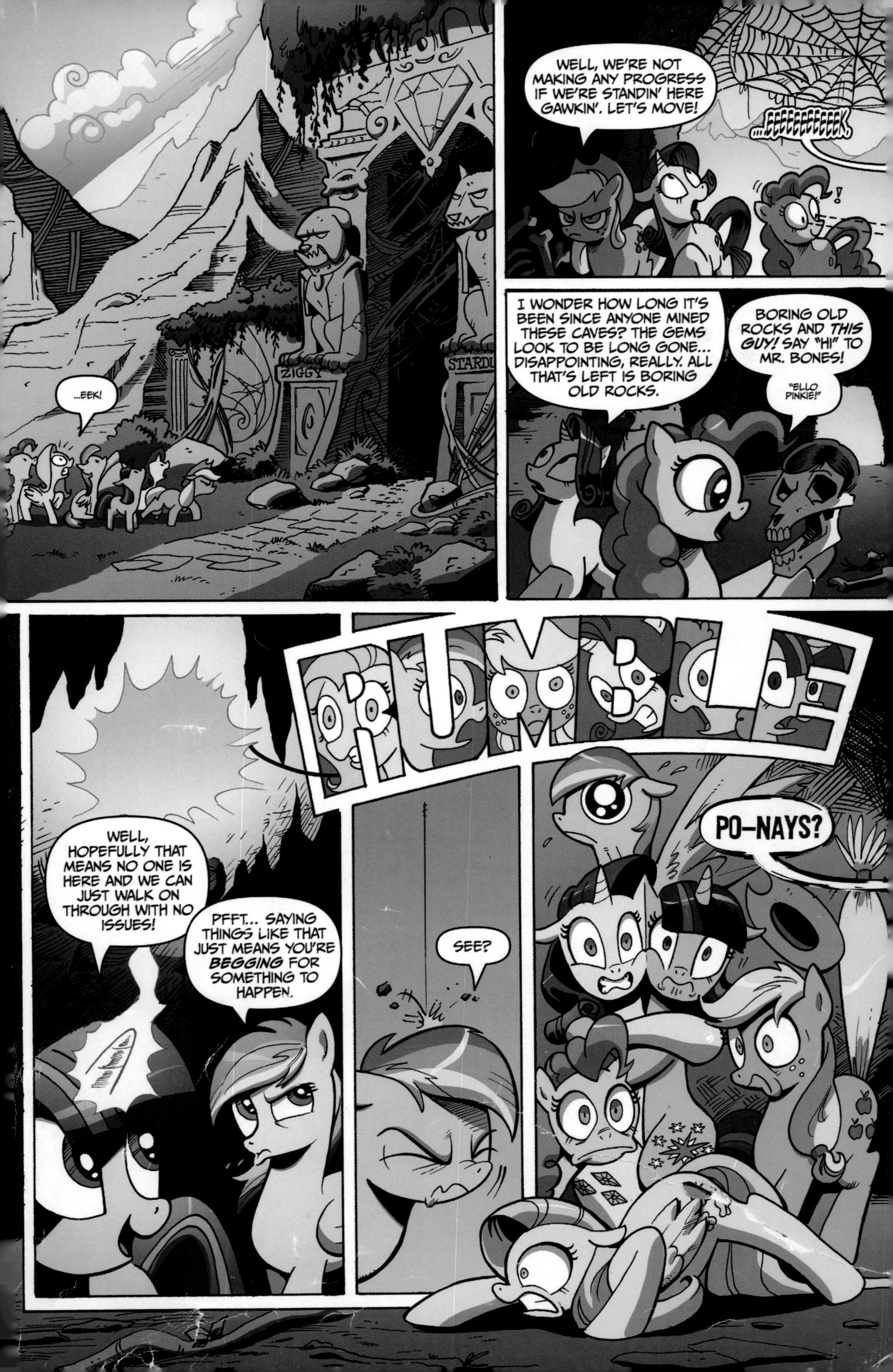
ZIGGY
STARDU
...EEK!
WELL, WE'RE NOT MAKING ANY PROGRESS IF WE'RE STANDIN' HERE GAWKIN'. LET'S MOVE!
...EEEEEEEEEEEK.
!
I WONDER HOW LONG IT'S BEEN SINCE ANYONE MINED THESE CAVES? THE GEMS LOOK TO BE LONG GONE... DISAPPOINTING, REALLY. ALL THAT'S LEFT IS BORING OLD ROCKS.
BORING OLD ROCKS AND THIS GUY! SAY "HI" TO MR. BONES!
"ELLO PINKIE!"
WELL, HOPEFULLY THAT MEANS NO ONE IS HERE AND WE CAN JUST WALK ON THROUGH WITH NO ISSUES!
PFFT... SAYING THINGS LIKE THAT JUST MEANS YOU'RE BEGGING FOR SOMETHING TO HAPPEN.
SEE?
RUMBLE
PO-NAYS?

PO-NAYS!

PWETAH PONAY!

EEK!

A *CAVE TROLL!* HOW EXCITING! THEY'RE MUCH BIGGER THAN THE "CAVE DWELLER'S REFERENCE GUIDE" SAYS THEY ARE!

EXCITING? WHAT IS *WRONG* WITH YOU?

PWETAH HAR ON DAH PWETAH PONAY

Brush
Brush

WELL THAT'S... ER... STRANGE.

HEY! PUT HER DOWN YA' BIG LUG!

YES! PUT HER DOWN THIS INSTANT! JUST LOOK WHAT YOU'RE DOING TO HER POOR MANE!

NEXT PONAY!

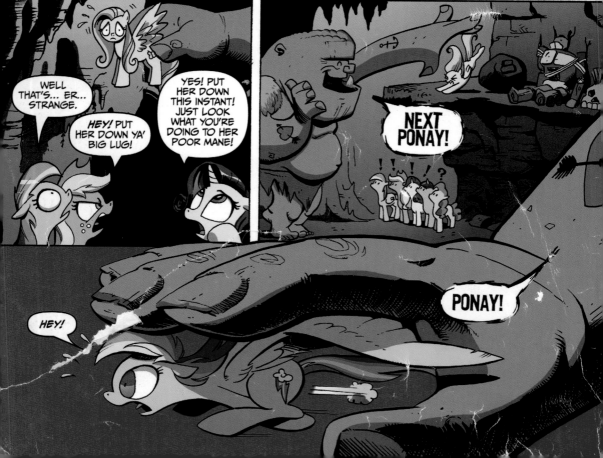

HEY!

PONAY!

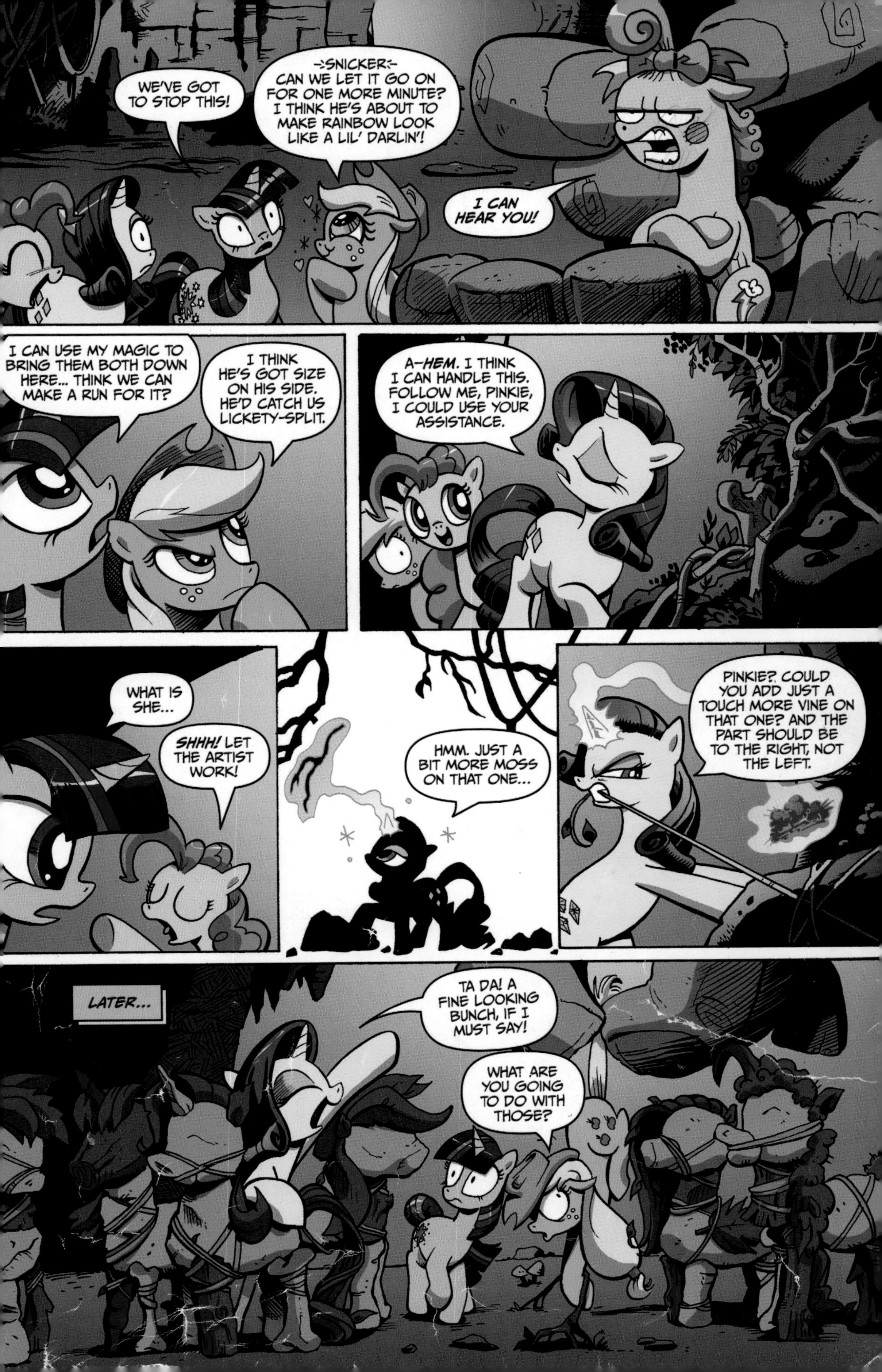
WE'VE GOT TO STOP THIS!
-SNICKER- CAN WE LET IT GO ON FOR ONE MORE MINUTE? I THINK HE'S ABOUT TO MAKE RAINBOW LOOK LIKE A LIL' DARLIN'!
I CAN HEAR YOU!
I CAN USE MY MAGIC TO BRING THEM BOTH DOWN HERE... THINK WE CAN MAKE A RUN FOR IT?
I THINK HE'S GOT SIZE ON HIS SIDE. HE'D CATCH US LICKETY-SPLIT.
A-HEM. I THINK I CAN HANDLE THIS. FOLLOW ME, PINKIE, I COULD USE YOUR ASSISTANCE.
WHAT IS SHE...
SHHH! LET THE ARTIST WORK!
HMM. JUST A BIT MORE MOSS ON THAT ONE...
PINKIE? COULD YOU ADD JUST A TOUCH MORE VINE ON THAT ONE? AND THE PART SHOULD BE TO THE RIGHT, NOT THE LEFT.
LATER...
TA DA! A FINE LOOKING BUNCH, IF I MUST SAY!
WHAT ARE YOU GOING TO DO WITH THOSE?

WATCH AND LEARN.

OH MR. TROOOOOOOOOOOLL... I HAVE A SURPRISE FOR YOU!

GASP! PONAYS!

AWW! HE HAS NEW FRIENDS!

I WIW CAWL DIS ONE GEORGE

GEORGE?!

COME ON, EVERY PONY. LET'S GET OUT OF HERE WHILE HE'S DISTRACTED.

BUT... BUT...

COME ON, GEORGE!

HE WASN'T REALLY A *BAD* LUMBERING BEAST, WAS HE?

HE DID GET BITS OF STICK STUCK IN YOUR MANE. THAT'S A RATHER BEASTLY THING, IF YOU ASK ME.

I CAN'T WAIT TO ADD THAT CAVE TROLLS LOVE TOYS TO MY REFERENCE BOOKS. A PERSONAL ENCOUNTER STORY ALWAYS ADDS TO THE EXCITEMENT OF A RESEARCH PAPER!

DID YOU JUST USE THE WORDS "EXCITEMENT" AND "RESEARCH" IN THE *SAME* SENTENCE?

LET'S CHECK WHERE WE ARE ON THE MAP. I BET WE'RE ALMOST HALFWAY THROUGH THE MOUNTAIN!

WELL, THAT WASN'T VERY EXCITING. WAS

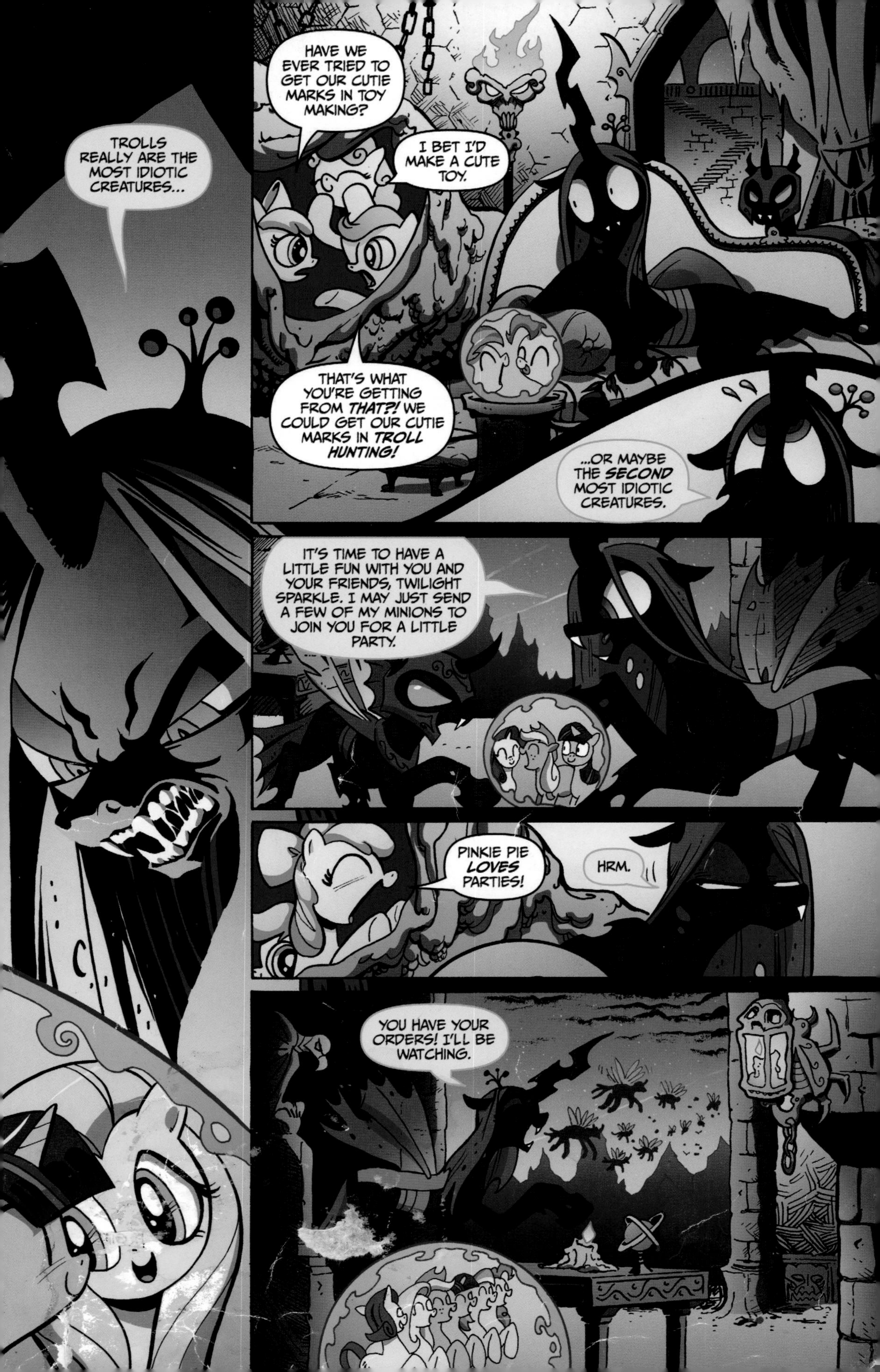
TROLLS REALLY ARE THE MOST IDIOTIC CREATURES...
HAVE WE EVER TRIED TO GET OUR CUTIE MARKS IN TOY MAKING?
I BET I'D MAKE A CUTE TOY.
THAT'S WHAT YOU'RE GETTING FROM *THAT?!* WE COULD GET OUR CUTIE MARKS IN *TROLL HUNTING!*
...OR MAYBE THE *SECOND* MOST IDIOTIC CREATURES.
IT'S TIME TO HAVE A LITTLE FUN WITH YOU AND YOUR FRIENDS, TWILIGHT SPARKLE. I MAY JUST SEND A FEW OF MY MINIONS TO JOIN YOU FOR A LITTLE PARTY.
PINKIE PIE *LOVES* PARTIES!
HRM.
YOU HAVE YOUR ORDERS! I'LL BE WATCHING.

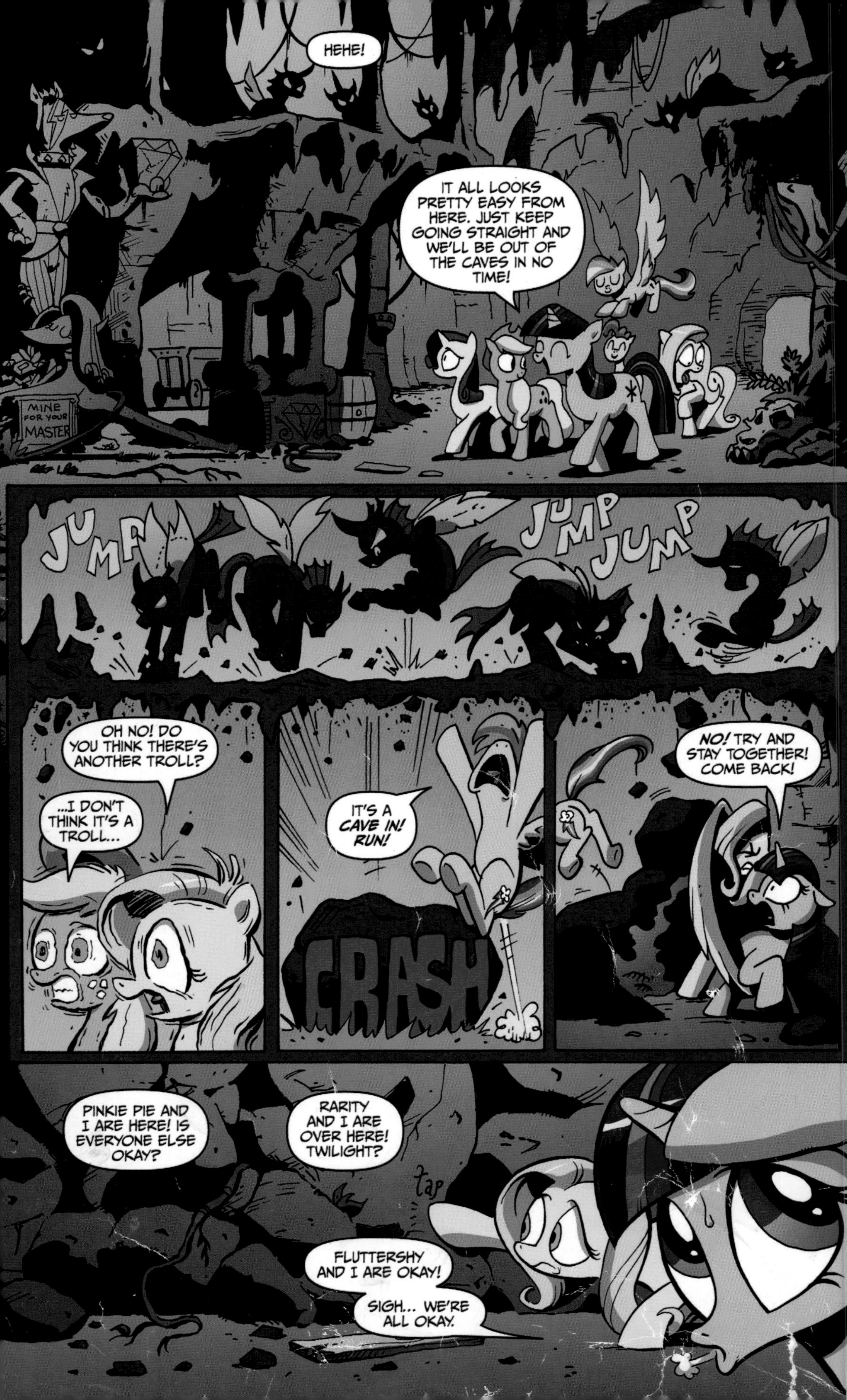
HEHE!
MINE FOR YOUR MASTER
IT ALL LOOKS PRETTY EASY FROM HERE. JUST KEEP GOING STRAIGHT AND WE'LL BE OUT OF THE CAVES IN NO TIME!
JUMP
JUMP JUMP
OH NO! DO YOU THINK THERE'S ANOTHER TROLL?
...I DON'T THINK IT'S A TROLL...
IT'S A CAVE IN! RUN!
CRASH
NO! TRY AND STAY TOGETHER! COME BACK!
PINKIE PIE AND I ARE HERE! IS EVERYONE ELSE OKAY?
RARITY AND I ARE OVER HERE! TWILIGHT?
tap
FLUTTERSHY AND I ARE OKAY!
SIGH... WE'RE ALL OKAY.

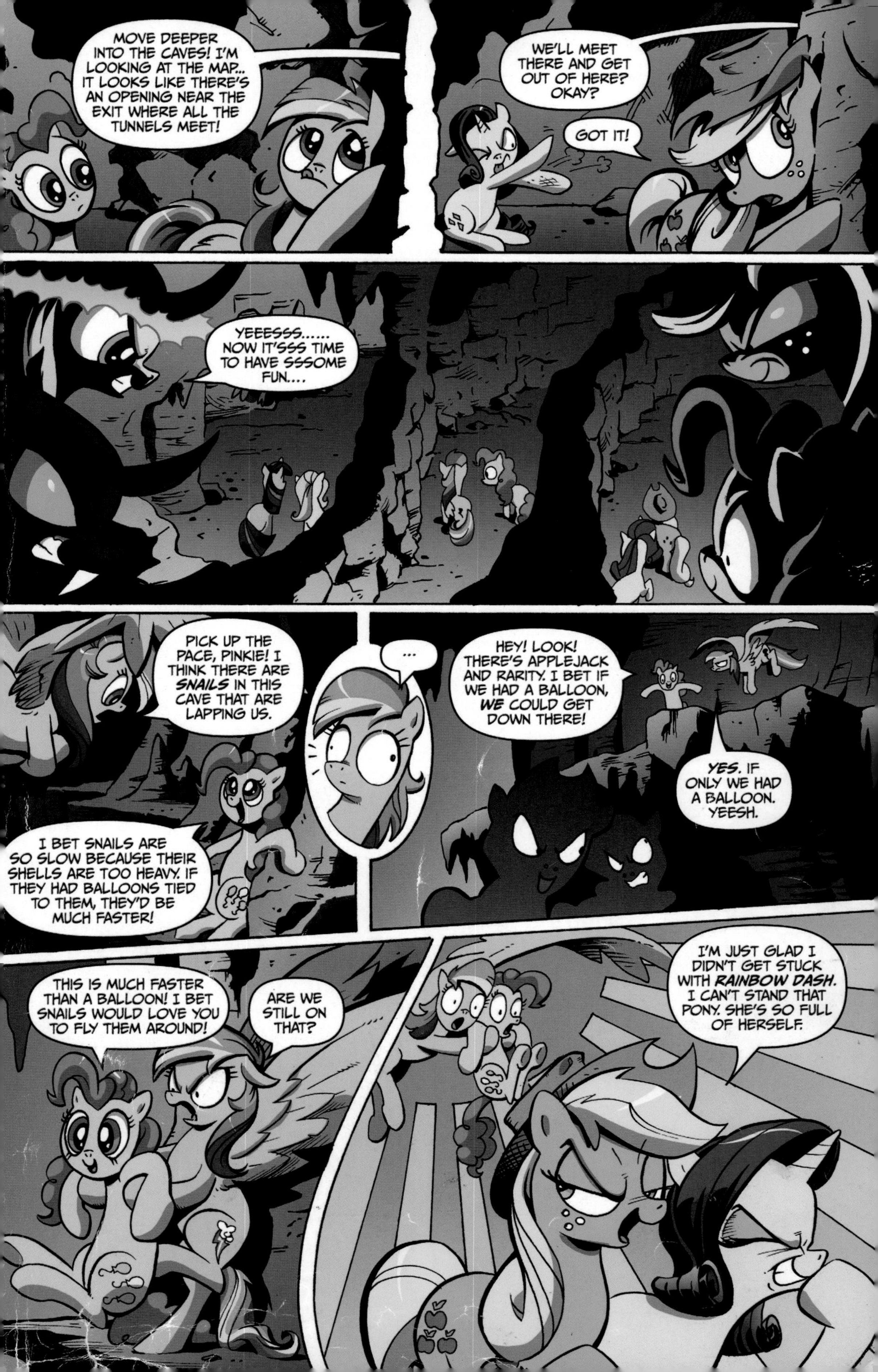
MOVE DEEPER INTO THE CAVES! I'M LOOKING AT THE MAP... IT LOOKS LIKE THERE'S AN OPENING NEAR THE EXIT WHERE ALL THE TUNNELS MEET!
WE'LL MEET THERE AND GET OUT OF HERE? OKAY?
GOT IT!
YEEESSS...... NOW IT'SSS TIME TO HAVE SSSOME FUN....
PICK UP THE PACE, PINKIE! I THINK THERE ARE *SNAILS* IN THIS CAVE THAT ARE LAPPING US.
I BET SNAILS ARE SO SLOW BECAUSE THEIR SHELLS ARE TOO HEAVY. IF THEY HAD BALLOONS TIED TO THEM, THEY'D BE MUCH FASTER!
...
HEY! LOOK! THERE'S APPLEJACK AND RARITY. I BET IF WE HAD A BALLOON, *WE* COULD GET DOWN THERE!
YES. IF ONLY WE HAD A BALLOON. YEESH.
THIS IS MUCH FASTER THAN A BALLOON! I BET SNAILS WOULD LOVE YOU TO FLY THEM AROUND!
ARE WE STILL ON THAT?
I'M JUST GLAD I DIDN'T GET STUCK WITH *RAINBOW DASH.* I CAN'T STAND THAT PONY. SHE'S SO FULL OF HERSELF.

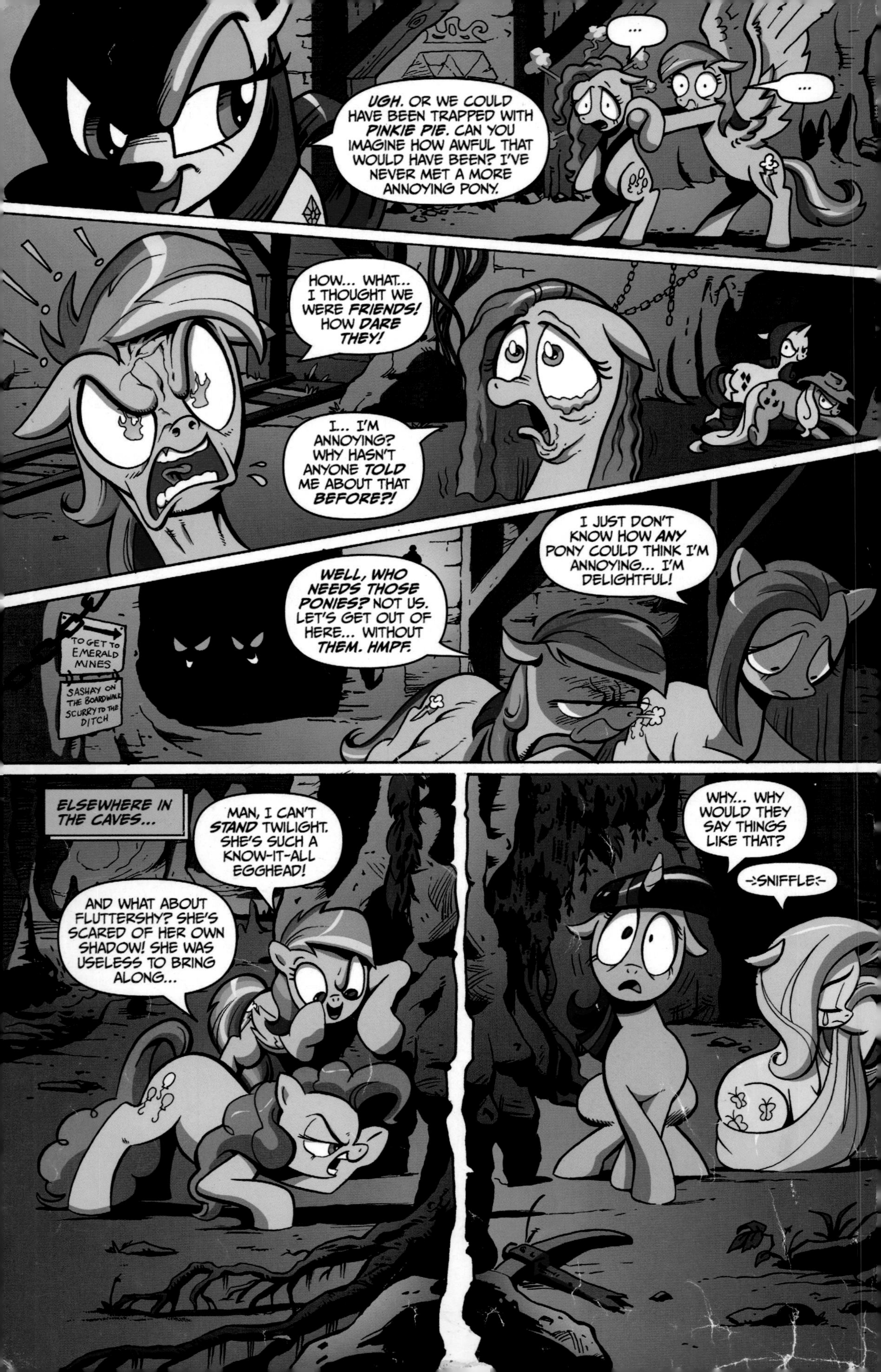
UGH. OR WE COULD HAVE BEEN TRAPPED WITH PINKIE PIE. CAN YOU IMAGINE HOW AWFUL THAT WOULD HAVE BEEN? I'VE NEVER MET A MORE ANNOYING PONY.
...
...
HOW... WHAT... I THOUGHT WE WERE FRIENDS! HOW DARE THEY!
I... I'M ANNOYING? WHY HASN'T ANYONE TOLD ME ABOUT THAT BEFORE?!
TO GET TO EMERALD MINES
SASHAY ON THE BOARDWALK SCURRY TO THE DITCH
WELL, WHO NEEDS THOSE PONIES? NOT US. LET'S GET OUT OF HERE... WITHOUT THEM. HMPF.
I JUST DON'T KNOW HOW ANY PONY COULD THINK I'M ANNOYING... I'M DELIGHTFUL!
ELSEWHERE IN THE CAVES...
MAN, I CAN'T STAND TWILIGHT. SHE'S SUCH A KNOW-IT-ALL EGGHEAD!
AND WHAT ABOUT FLUTTERSHY? SHE'S SCARED OF HER OWN SHADOW! SHE WAS USELESS TO BRING ALONG...
WHY... WHY WOULD THEY SAY THINGS LIKE THAT?
-SNIFFLE-

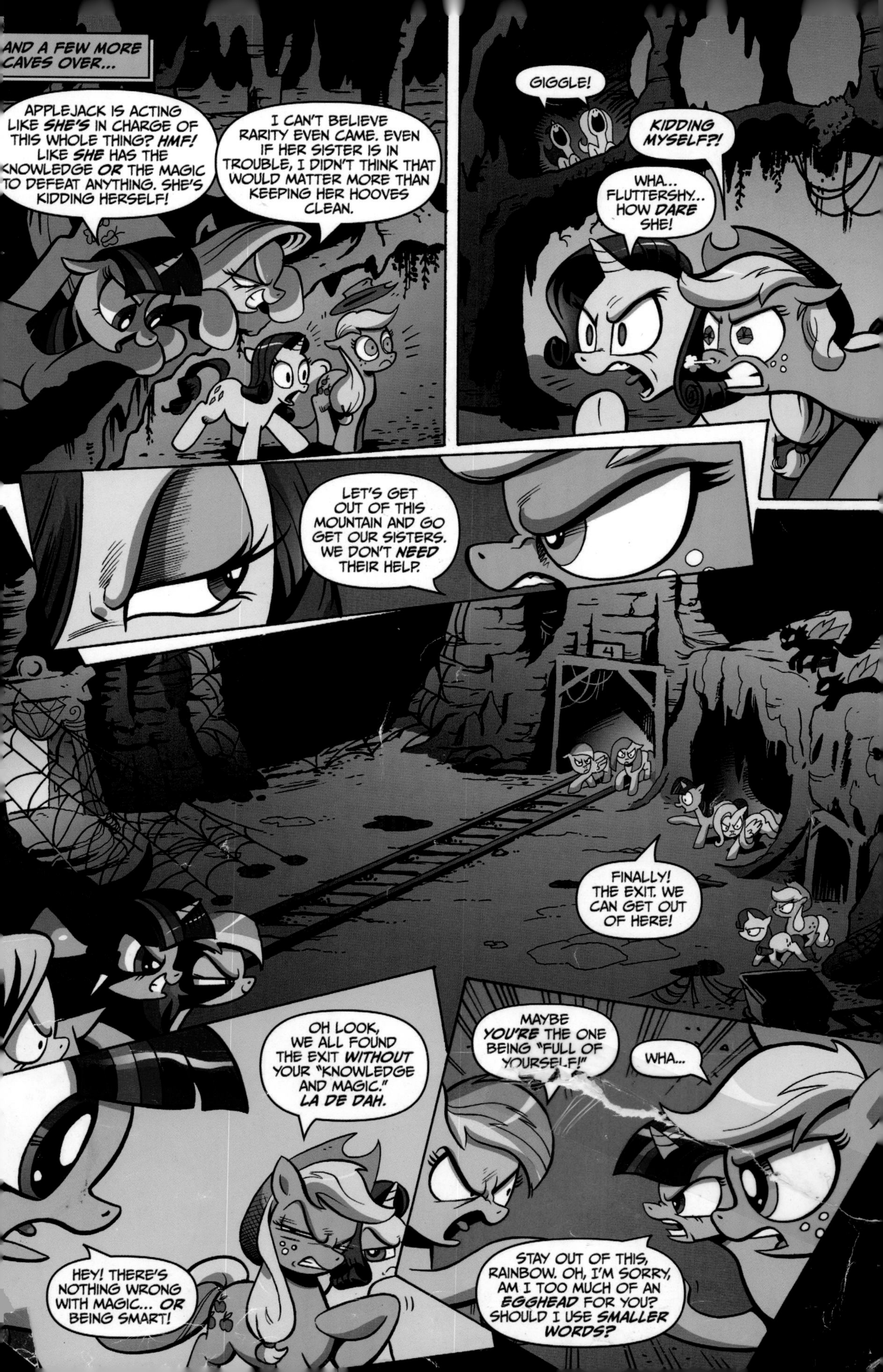
AND A FEW MORE CAVES OVER...
APPLEJACK IS ACTING LIKE SHE'S IN CHARGE OF THIS WHOLE THING? HMF! LIKE SHE HAS THE KNOWLEDGE OR THE MAGIC TO DEFEAT ANYTHING. SHE'S KIDDING HERSELF!
I CAN'T BELIEVE RARITY EVEN CAME. EVEN IF HER SISTER IS IN TROUBLE, I DIDN'T THINK THAT WOULD MATTER MORE THAN KEEPING HER HOOVES CLEAN.
GIGGLE!
KIDDING MYSELF?!
WHA... FLUTTERSHY... HOW DARE SHE!
LET'S GET OUT OF THIS MOUNTAIN AND GO GET OUR SISTERS. WE DON'T NEED THEIR HELP.
4
FINALLY! THE EXIT. WE CAN GET OUT OF HERE!
OH LOOK, WE ALL FOUND THE EXIT WITHOUT YOUR "KNOWLEDGE AND MAGIC." LA DE DAH.
MAYBE YOU'RE THE ONE BEING "FULL OF YOURSELF!"
WHA...
HEY! THERE'S NOTHING WRONG WITH MAGIC... OR BEING SMART!
STAY OUT OF THIS, RAINBOW. OH, I'M SORRY, AM I TOO MUCH OF AN EGGHEAD FOR YOU? SHOULD I USE SMALLER WORDS?

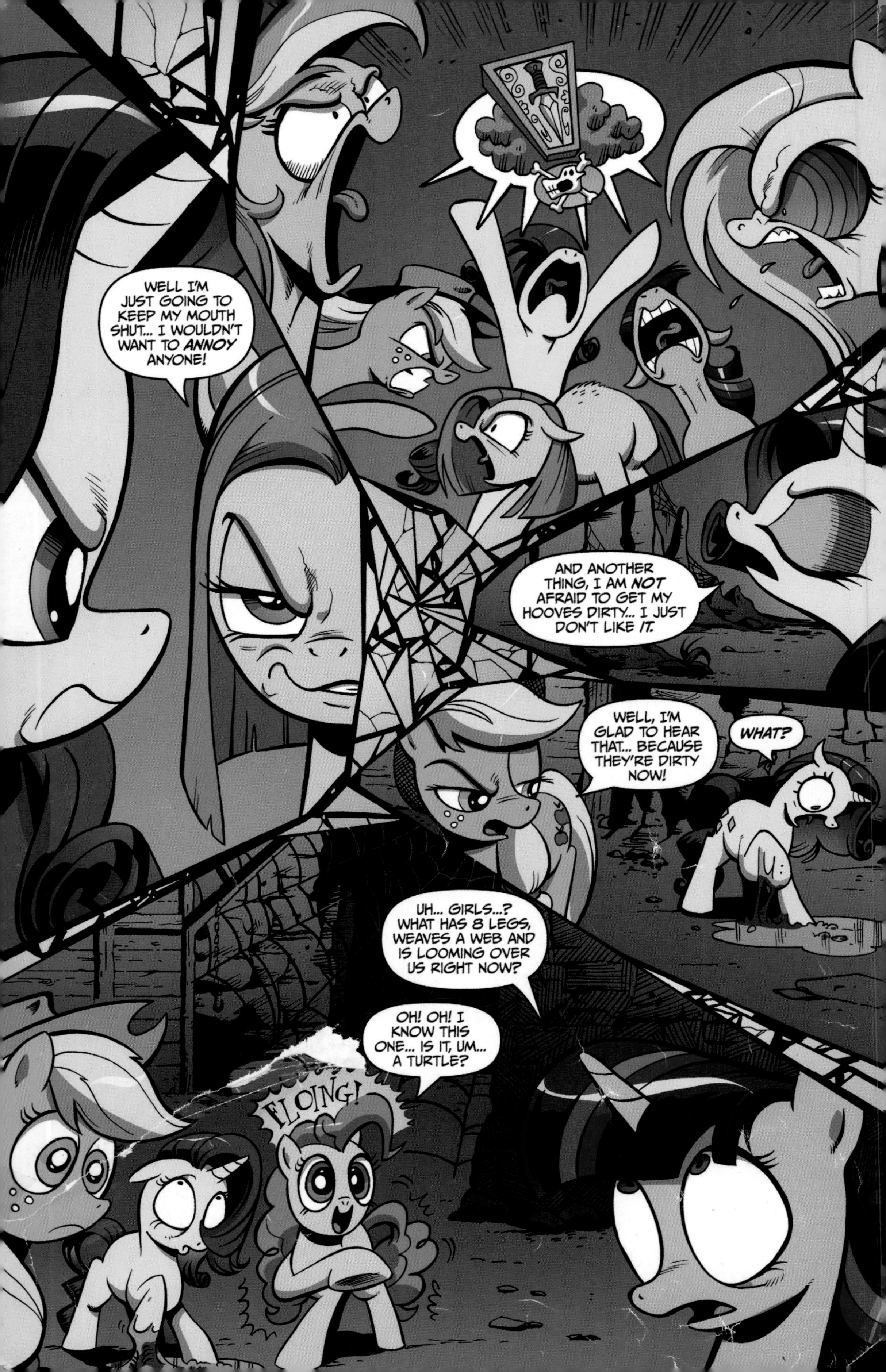
WELL I'M JUST GOING TO KEEP MY MOUTH SHUT... I WOULDN'T WANT TO *ANNOY* ANYONE!
AND ANOTHER THING, I AM *NOT* AFRAID TO GET MY HOOVES DIRTY... I JUST DON'T LIKE *IT.*
WELL, I'M GLAD TO HEAR THAT... BECAUSE THEY'RE DIRTY NOW!
WHAT?
UH... GIRLS...? WHAT HAS 8 LEGS, WEAVES A WEB AND IS LOOMING OVER US RIGHT NOW?
OH! OH! I KNOW THIS ONE... IS IT, UM... A TURTLE?
FLOING!

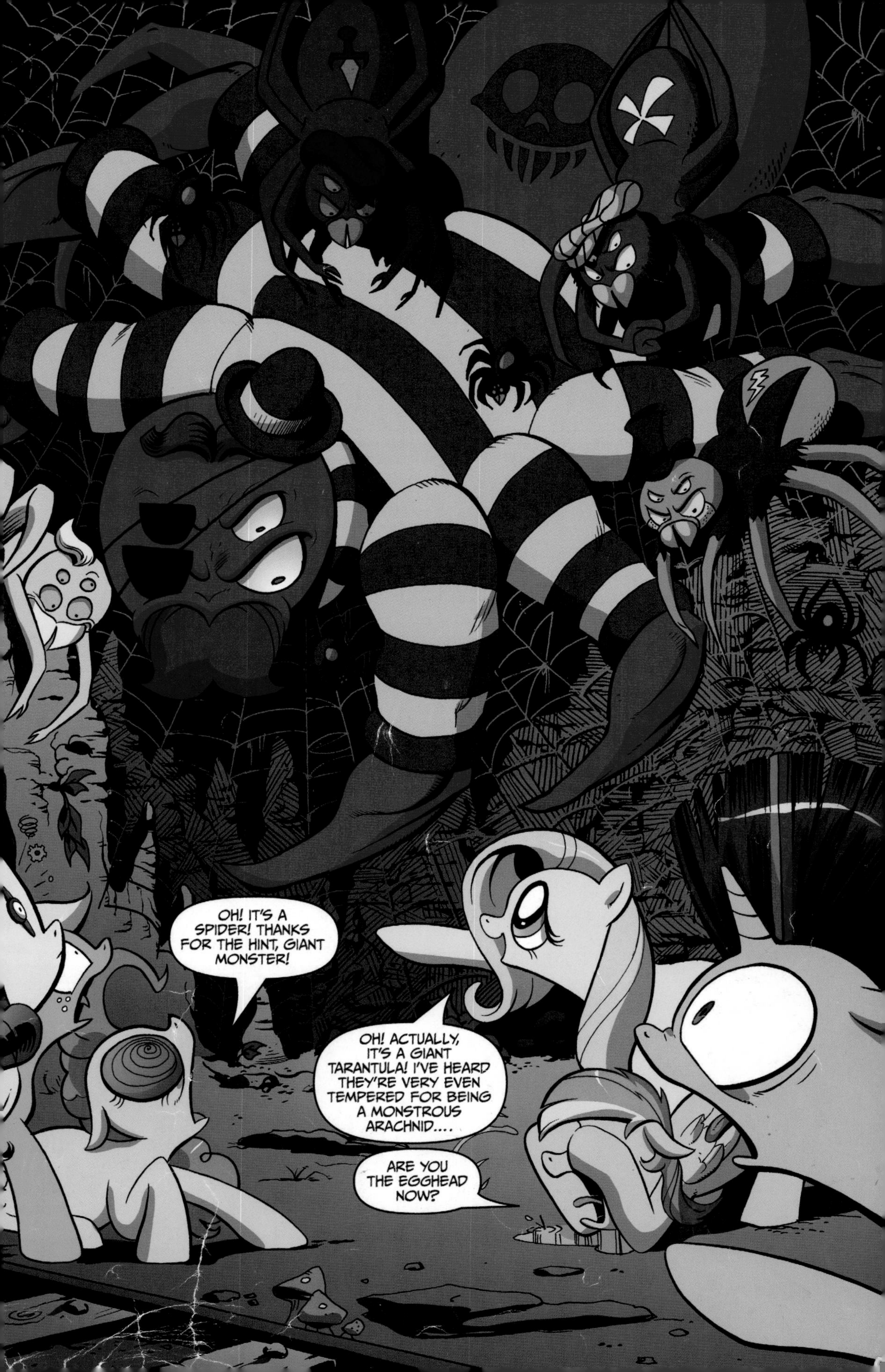
OH! IT'S A SPIDER! THANKS FOR THE HINT, GIANT MONSTER!
OH! ACTUALLY, IT'S A GIANT TARANTULA! I'VE HEARD THEY'RE VERY EVEN TEMPERED FOR BEING A MONSTROUS ARACHNID....
ARE YOU THE EGGHEAD NOW?

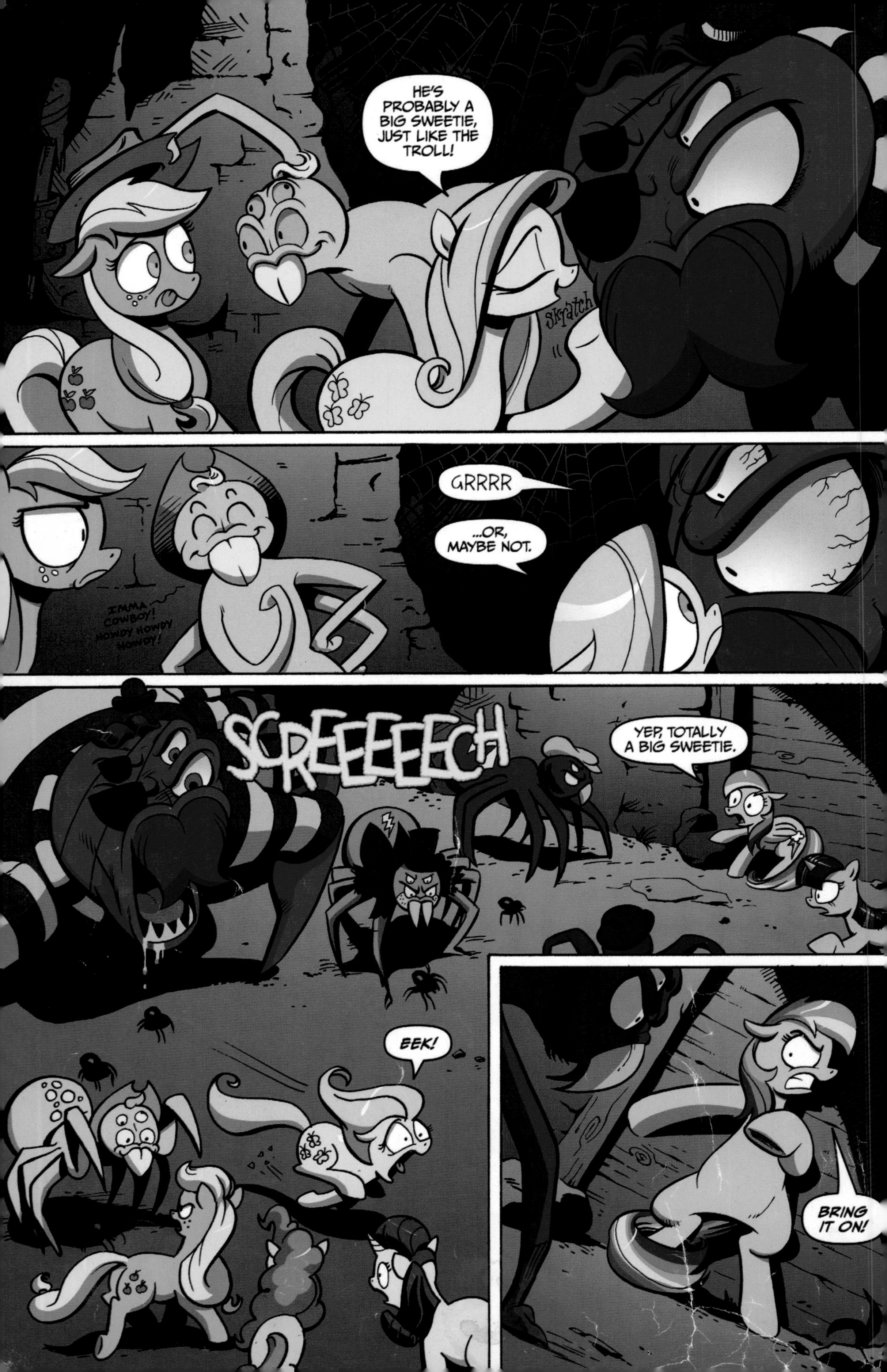
HE'S PROBABLY A BIG SWEETIE, JUST LIKE THE TROLL!
SKRATCH
GRRRR
...OR, MAYBE NOT.
IMMA COWBOY! HOWDY HOWDY HOWDY!
SCREEEEEECH
YEP, TOTALLY A BIG SWEETIE.
EEK!
BRING IT ON!

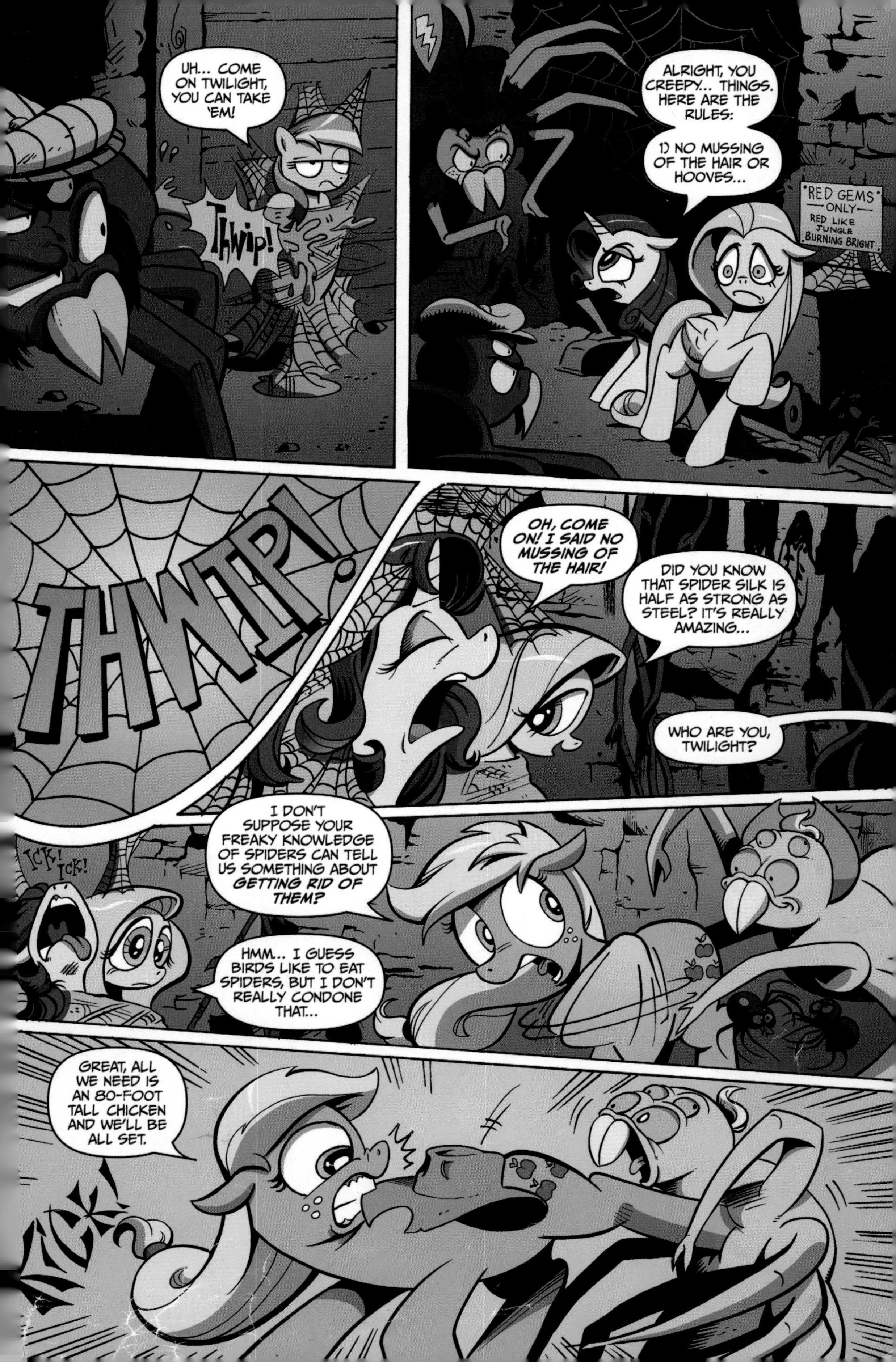
UH... COME ON TWILIGHT, YOU CAN TAKE 'EM!
THWIP!
ALRIGHT, YOU CREEPY... THINGS. HERE ARE THE RULES:
1) NO MUSSING OF THE HAIR OR HOOVES...
RED GEMS ONLY RED LIKE JUNGLE BURNING BRIGHT
THWIP!
OH, COME ON! I SAID NO MUSSING OF THE HAIR!
DID YOU KNOW THAT SPIDER SILK IS HALF AS STRONG AS STEEL? IT'S REALLY AMAZING...
WHO ARE YOU, TWILIGHT?
ICK! ICK!
I DON'T SUPPOSE YOUR FREAKY KNOWLEDGE OF SPIDERS CAN TELL US SOMETHING ABOUT *GETTING RID OF THEM?*
HMM... I GUESS BIRDS LIKE TO EAT SPIDERS, BUT I DON'T REALLY CONDONE THAT...
GREAT, ALL WE NEED IS AN 80-FOOT TALL CHICKEN AND WE'LL BE ALL SET.

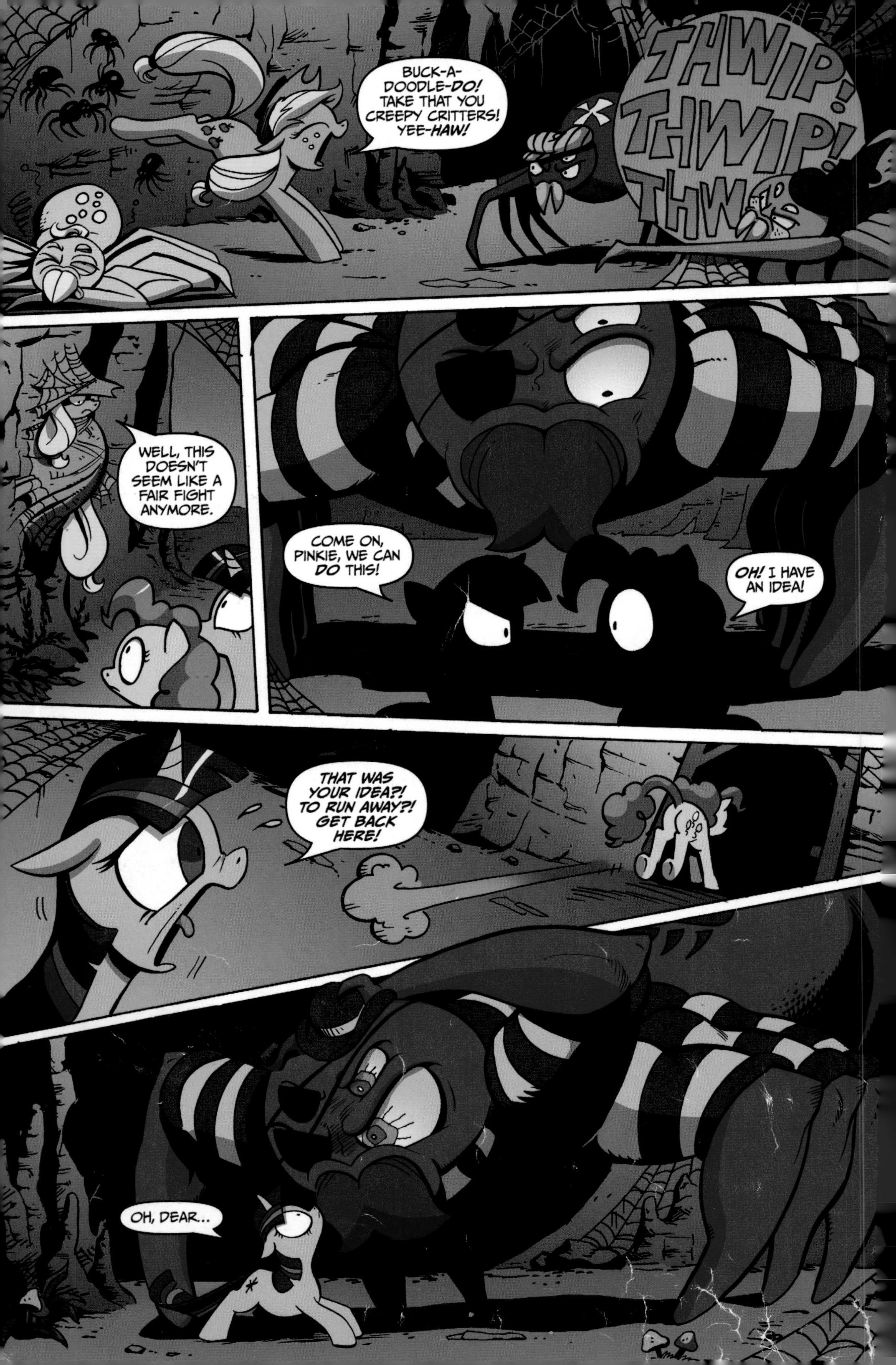
BUCK-A-DOODLE-DO! TAKE THAT YOU CREEPY CRITTERS! YEE-HAW!
THWIP! THWIP! THW
WELL, THIS DOESN'T SEEM LIKE A FAIR FIGHT ANYMORE.
COME ON, PINKIE, WE CAN DO THIS!
OH! I HAVE AN IDEA!
THAT WAS YOUR IDEA?! TO RUN AWAY?! GET BACK HERE!
OH, DEAR...

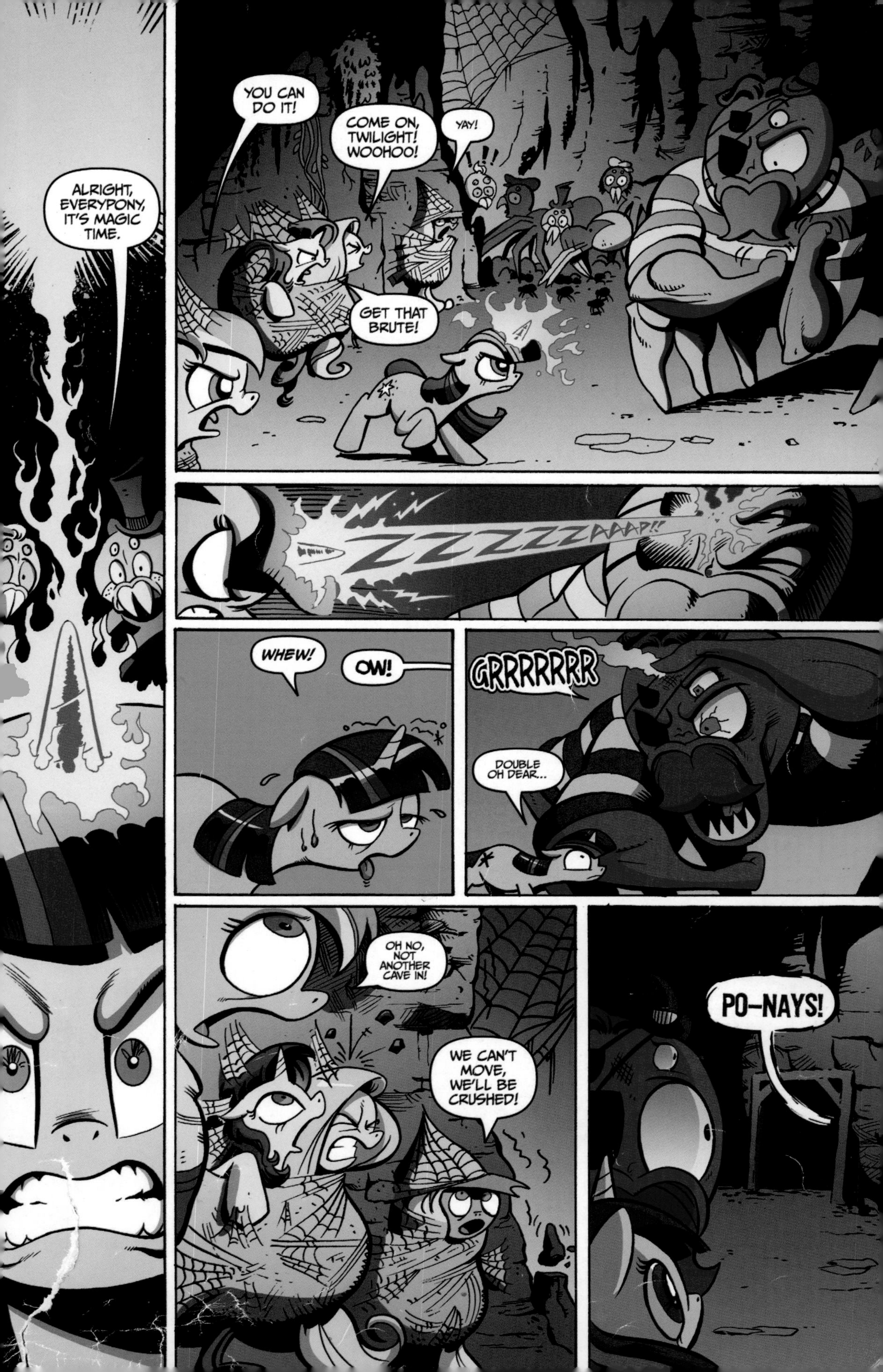
ALRIGHT, EVERYPONY, IT'S MAGIC TIME.
YOU CAN DO IT!
COME ON, TWILIGHT! WOOHOO!
YAY!
GET THAT BRUTE!
ZZZZZZZAAAP!!
WHEW!
OW!
GRRRRRRR
DOUBLE OH DEAR...
OH NO, NOT ANOTHER CAVE IN!
WE CAN'T MOVE, WE'LL BE CRUSHED!
PO-NAYS!

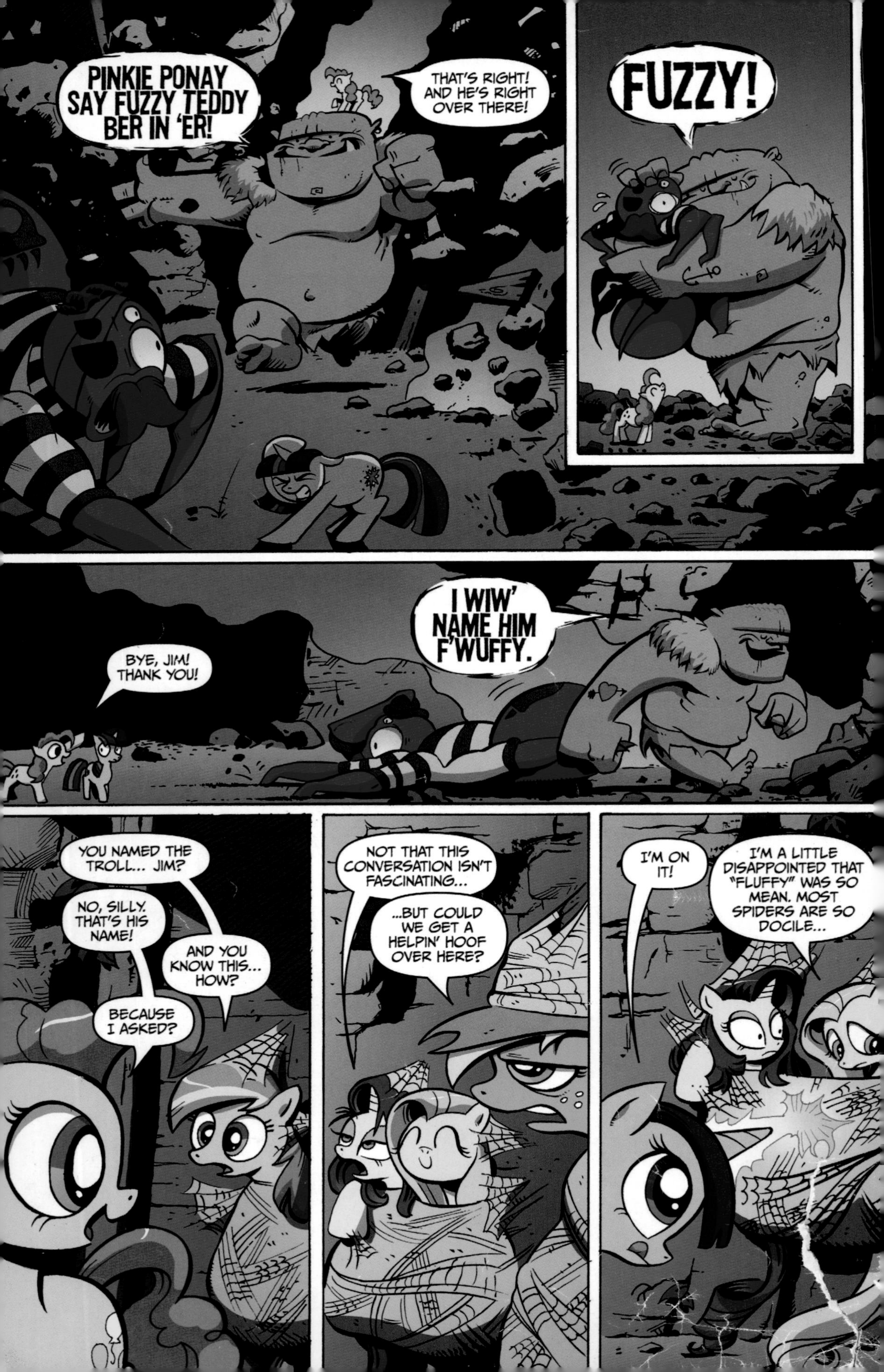
PINKIE PONAY SAY FUZZY TEDDY BER IN 'ER!
THAT'S RIGHT! AND HE'S RIGHT OVER THERE!
FUZZY!
I WIW' NAME HIM F'WUFFY.
BYE, JIM! THANK YOU!
YOU NAMED THE TROLL... JIM?
NO, SILLY. THAT'S HIS NAME!
AND YOU KNOW THIS... HOW?
BECAUSE I ASKED?
NOT THAT THIS CONVERSATION ISN'T FASCINATING...
...BUT COULD WE GET A HELPIN' HOOF OVER HERE?
I'M ON IT!
I'M A LITTLE DISAPPOINTED THAT "FLUFFY" WAS SO MEAN. MOST SPIDERS ARE SO DOCILE...

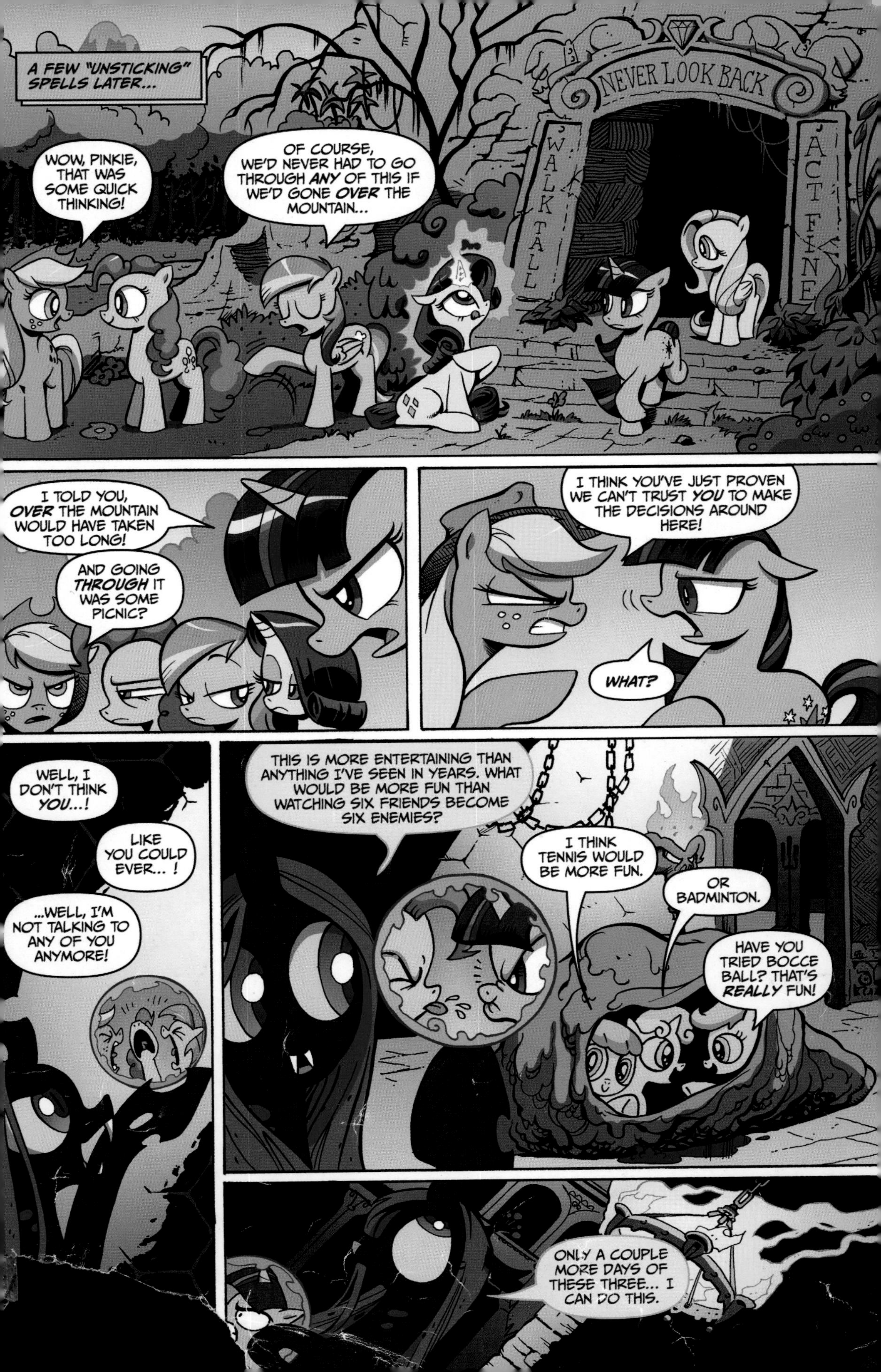
A FEW "UNSTICKING" SPELLS LATER...
NEVER LOOK BACK
WALK TALL
ACT FINE
WOW, PINKIE, THAT WAS SOME QUICK THINKING!
OF COURSE, WE'D NEVER HAD TO GO THROUGH ANY OF THIS IF WE'D GONE OVER THE MOUNTAIN...
I TOLD YOU, OVER THE MOUNTAIN WOULD HAVE TAKEN TOO LONG!
AND GOING THROUGH IT WAS SOME PICNIC?
I THINK YOU'VE JUST PROVEN WE CAN'T TRUST YOU TO MAKE THE DECISIONS AROUND HERE!
WHAT?
WELL, I DON'T THINK YOU...!
LIKE YOU COULD EVER... !
...WELL, I'M NOT TALKING TO ANY OF YOU ANYMORE!
THIS IS MORE ENTERTAINING THAN ANYTHING I'VE SEEN IN YEARS. WHAT WOULD BE MORE FUN THAN WATCHING SIX FRIENDS BECOME SIX ENEMIES?
I THINK TENNIS WOULD BE MORE FUN.
OR BADMINTON.
HAVE YOU TRIED BOCCE BALL? THAT'S REALLY FUN!
ONLY A COUPLE MORE DAYS OF THESE THREE... I CAN DO THIS.

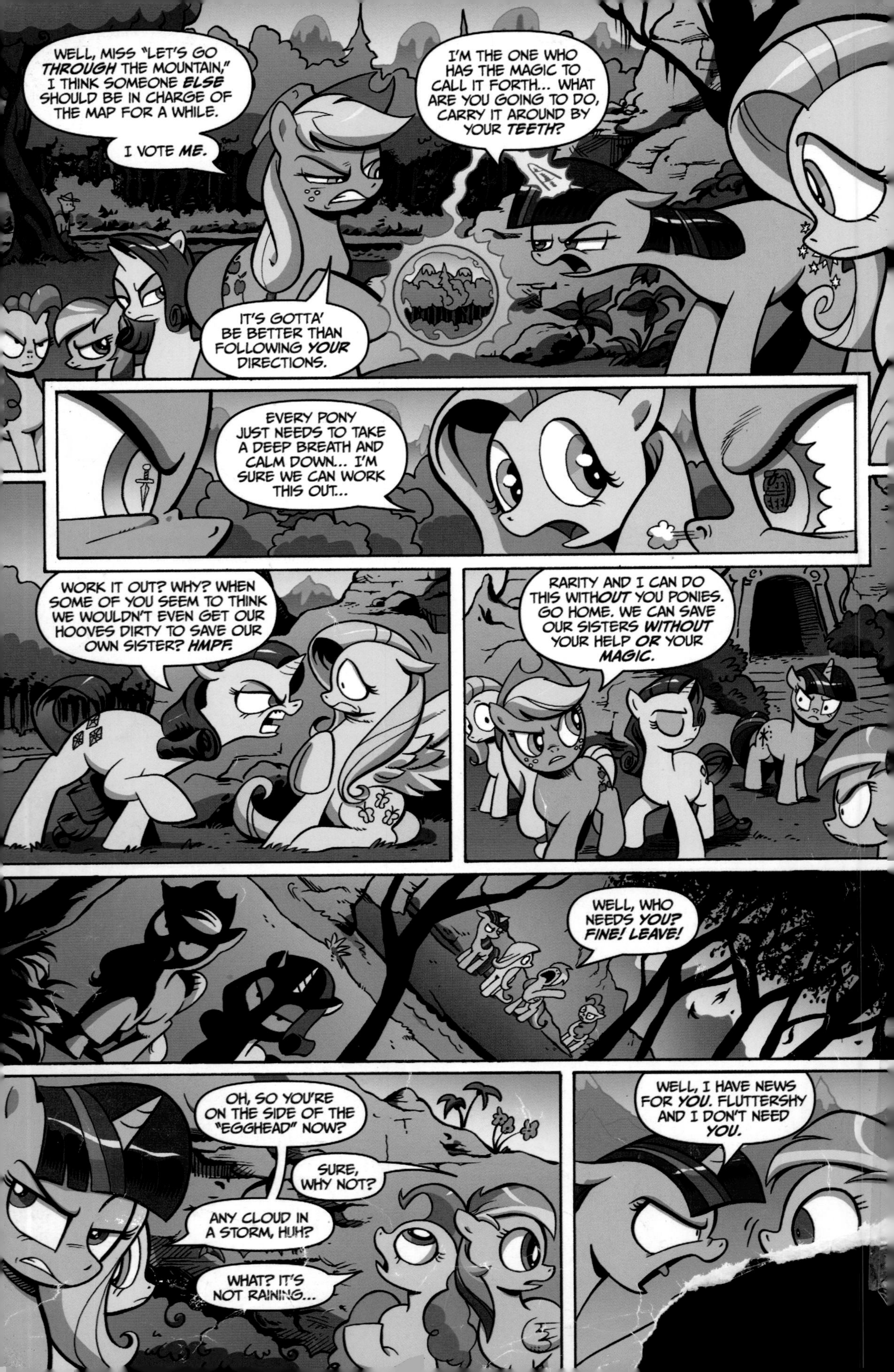
WELL, MISS "LET'S GO THROUGH THE MOUNTAIN," I THINK SOMEONE ELSE SHOULD BE IN CHARGE OF THE MAP FOR A WHILE.
I VOTE ME.
I'M THE ONE WHO HAS THE MAGIC TO CALL IT FORTH... WHAT ARE YOU GOING TO DO, CARRY IT AROUND BY YOUR TEETH?
IT'S GOTTA' BE BETTER THAN FOLLOWING YOUR DIRECTIONS.
EVERY PONY JUST NEEDS TO TAKE A DEEP BREATH AND CALM DOWN... I'M SURE WE CAN WORK THIS OUT...
WORK IT OUT? WHY? WHEN SOME OF YOU SEEM TO THINK WE WOULDN'T EVEN GET OUR HOOVES DIRTY TO SAVE OUR OWN SISTER? HMPF.
RARITY AND I CAN DO THIS WITHOUT YOU PONIES. GO HOME. WE CAN SAVE OUR SISTERS WITHOUT YOUR HELP OR YOUR MAGIC.
WELL, WHO NEEDS YOU? FINE! LEAVE!
OH, SO YOU'RE ON THE SIDE OF THE "EGGHEAD" NOW?
SURE, WHY NOT?
ANY CLOUD IN A STORM, HUH?
WHAT? IT'S NOT RAINING...
WELL, I HAVE NEWS FOR YOU. FLUTTERSHY AND I DON'T NEED YOU.

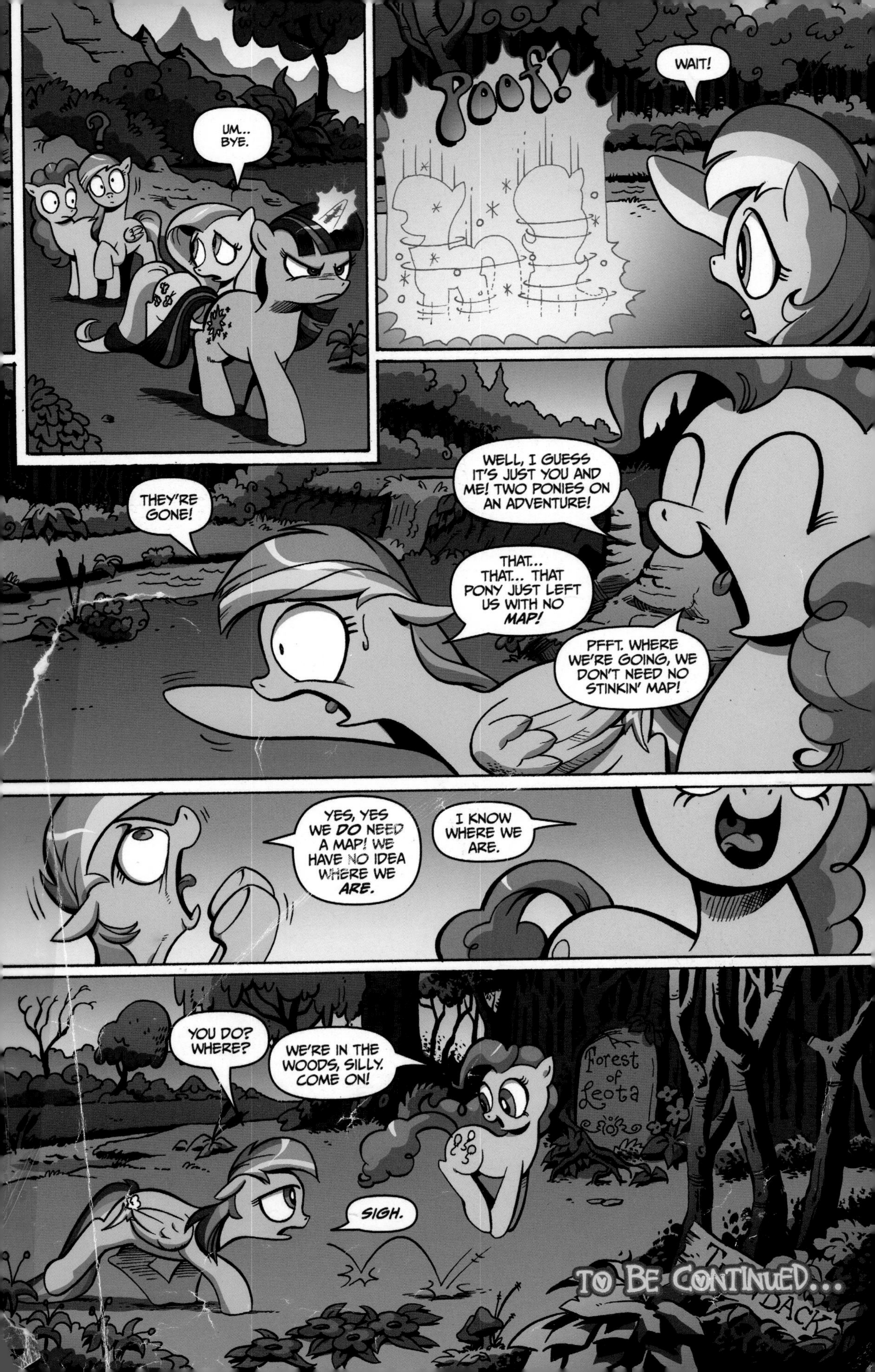
UM.. BYE.
POOF!
WAIT!
THEY'RE GONE!
WELL, I GUESS IT'S JUST YOU AND ME! TWO PONIES ON AN ADVENTURE!
THAT... THAT... THAT PONY JUST LEFT US WITH NO MAP!
PFFT. WHERE WE'RE GOING, WE DON'T NEED NO STINKIN' MAP!
YES, YES WE DO NEED A MAP! WE HAVE NO IDEA WHERE WE ARE.
I KNOW WHERE WE ARE.
YOU DO? WHERE?
WE'RE IN THE WOODS, SILLY. COME ON!
Forest of Leota
SIGH.
TO BE CONTINUED...

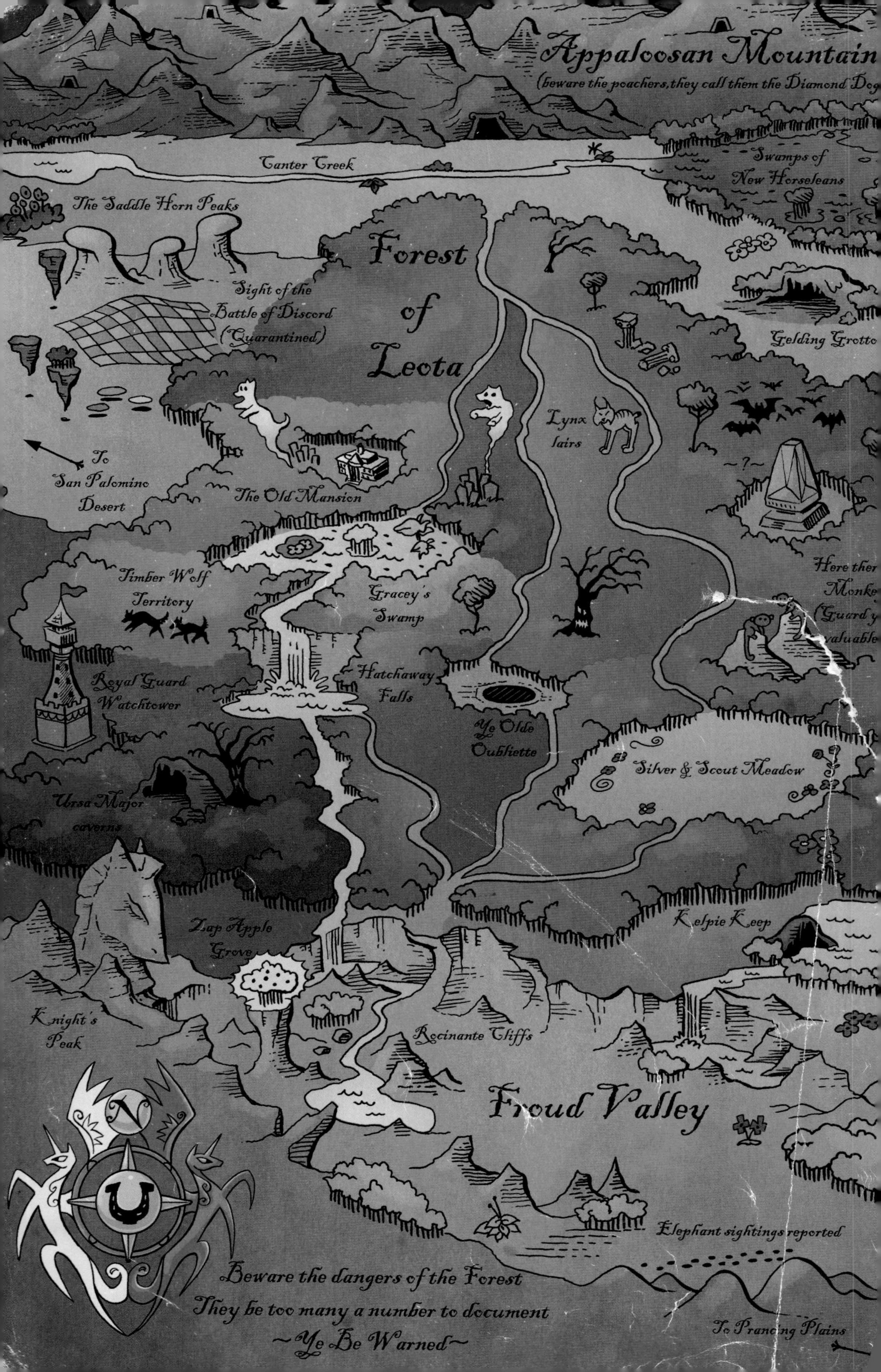

Appaloosan Mountain
(beware the poachers, they call them the Diamond Dog
Canter Creek
Swamps of
New Horseleans
The Saddle Horn Peaks
Forest
of
Leota
Sight of the
Battle of Discord
(Quarantined)
Gelding Grotto
Lynx
lairs
To
San Palomino
Desert
The Old Mansion
~?~
Here ther
Monke
(Guard y
valuable
Timber Wolf
Territory
Gracey's
Swamp
Royal Guard
Watchtower
Hatchaway
Falls
Ye Olde
Oubliette
Silver & Scout Meadow
Ursa Major
caverns
Kelpie Keep
Zap Apple
Grove
Knight's
Peak
Rocinante Cliffs
N
Froud Valley
Elephant sightings reported
Beware the dangers of the Forest
They be too many a number to document
~Ye Be Warned~
To Prancing Plains